To baby Lili; her mother, Miriam;
and her grandparents Vicki and David
—M.E.

To my mom, Betty Arengi, who taught me to sew and laugh
and all kinds of other wonderful things. I love you, Ma.
—J.C.

Text copyright © 2012 by Michelle Edwards
Cover art and interior illustrations copyright © 2012 by Jana Christy

All rights reserved. Published in the United States by Random House Children's Books, a division of Random House, Inc., New York.

Random House and the colophon are registered trademarks of Random House, Inc.

Visit us on the Web! randomhouse.com/kids

Educators and librarians, for a variety of teaching tools, visit us at
randomhouse.com/teachers

ISBN 978-0-375-97250-8

MANUFACTURED IN CHINA
10 9 8 7 6 5 4 3 2 1
First Edition

Room for the Baby

by Michelle Edwards • illustrated by Jana Christy

RANDOM HOUSE NEW YORK

Once on 18th Avenue, when someone had something they didn't need anymore, they gave it to my mom. Worn-out sheets. Yarn left over from knitting a sweater. A bolt of flannel from a tailor shop that went out of business. Everyone knew Mom would put it all to good use.

With what she took, Mom made our curtains, our blankets—and even made herself a winter coat. What she didn't use right away, she saved for later. Mom filled our sewing room's corners, its nooks, and its crannies. Then something happened that changed everything.

One fine spring morning, as we buttered our Passover matzos,
Mom announced, "We are going to have a baby!"
Dad drew us together in a family hug.
"Where will the baby sleep?" I asked.

"The sewing room will be for the baby," said Mom. "I've always said I would use the things I saved. Now I will. You'll see."

But I was worried. Could Mom really use up all that stuff before the baby was born?

That afternoon, Dad carried the sewing machine to the dining room table. Mom and I gathered two big piles of worn-out sheets that our neighbor Mr. Liu had brought over a few months before.

All week, Mom tore and snipped and sewed. By Friday, as our Shabbat hallah came out of the oven, she'd made dozens of soft diapers for the baby.

"My daughter is expecting, too," said Mrs. Finkelstein
from next door. "She'll need diapers like yours."
I helped Mom bundle another batch of old sheets.

Now one corner was empty.
"There still isn't enough room," I told her.
"Patience," said Mom. "You'll see."
"What's next?" Dad asked.
Mom pointed to a tower of suitcases.

The rest of that spring, she unpacked all the pajamas that our downstairs neighbor's kids had worn when they were small. She took out the elastic, the snaps, and the seams. All summer, she cut and she pinned and she stitched.

That autumn on Rosh Hashanah, we had apples dipped in honey for a sweet New Year. And Mom had stacks of tiny sleepers and onesies and little shirts ready for the baby.

"Cute," said Mom's friend Mrs. Martinez. She had a two-year-old. So did Mrs. Liu. As did Mrs. Liu's sister, also named Mrs. Liu. Mom asked me to bring them the stash of basketball jerseys from the teams my uncle coached.

"My daughter needs some sleepers, too," said Mrs. Finkelstein. She was over again.

After the holiday, Mom sent me to dig out the lost-and-found box that the owner of the corner candy store had given us. Later when I twirled around and around and around in the sewing room, I didn't bump into anything.

"See?" said Mom.

"Progress is definitely being made," said Dad.

A few weeks later, just before Simhat Torah, Mom showed me how to make a flag from chopsticks and half a sweater sleeve. While she unraveled a steamer trunkful of holey sweaters and mismatched mittens, I made a flag with pom-poms and yarn streamers and tucked it away in my sock drawer.

After the unraveled yarn was washed and dried, I helped Mom roll
it into balls. The rest of that autumn, Mom knit and knit and knit.

That winter, on the first night of Hanukkah, it snowed. Mom had blankets for the baby and new mittens for Dad and me. When our upstairs neighbor Mrs. Mack brought us a plate of her homemade potato latkes, she stared at my mittens.

"My Norman's hands are always cold," she said.

Mom asked me to find the hatbox filled with balls of thick wool
and metal knitting needles that Mrs. Finkelstein had given her. Now
there were three empty corners. There was almost enough room for
the baby. But I wasn't worried anymore. I knew just what to do.

Early the next morning, Mrs. Maggio came and collected a stack
of magazines. Mrs. Finkelstein came and requested only socks.

She wouldn't tell me what they were for. Mr. Liu needed
empty wooden spools. He told me they were for a secret project.

By noon, our friends and neighbors on 18th Avenue had taken back most of what everyone had given Mom. Now there was room for the baby.

Dad carried in the crib he had built from the steamer trunk. I washed the windows while Mom made curtains from the flannel that Mr. Epstein had given her when he'd closed his tailor shop.

On the third night of Hanukkah, my sister Lily was born.
She was pink and perfect. And so was her room.

On the last night of Hanukkah, the two Mrs. Lius, Mr. Liu,
Mrs. Martinez, Mrs. Maggio, Mrs. Mack, and Mrs. Finkelstein
stopped by. Everyone had made a gift for Lily. And so had I.

Once on 18th Avenue, when someone had something they didn't need anymore, they gave it to my mom. Now we all know just what to do with worn sheets and socks and even empty wooden spools. We use and reuse it all, and sometimes we make something new.